A Palace Full of Princesses

A Palace Full of Princesses

Written and illustrated
by Sally Gardner

Orion
Children's Books

Contents

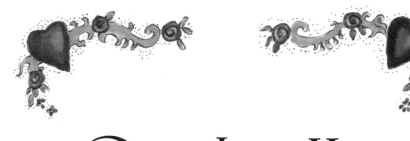

Cinderella

 # Contents

For Rosie Weber

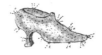

Chapter One

Once upon a time there lived a
beautiful girl called Cinderella.
Cinderella was not her real name,
but that was what her stepmother
and stepsisters called her.

When Cinderella's mother died,
her father was heartbroken. Then he
met a lady with two daughters of
Cinderella's age, who seemed to
be just what he needed.

In no time at all they were married.
Now Cinderella would have a kind
stepmother to look after her, and
two sweet stepsisters as well.
But oh dear me, how wrong
Cinderella's father was.

As soon as the wedding was over,
Cinderella was moved out of her bedroom
and down to the kitchen, where she was
to live and work as a servant.

Cinderella's stepmother was a jealous
woman with a wicked temper.

Cinderella's stepsisters, Henrietta and
Georgina, were spoilt, ugly girls who took
great delight in bullying Cinderella.

Their mother was determined that one
of her daughters should marry a prince,
so they had lessons in talking nicely,
walking nicely, and smiling nicely.

She gave them whatever they wanted,
but nothing made the two sisters
any happier or kinder.

The more they were given, the meaner
and nastier they became.

Nobody took any notice of Cinderella.
She just did the housework.

Her father could do nothing for her.
He was much too frightened
of his new wife.

Chapter Two

Time went on and
nothing changed.

To the fury of her stepmother
and stepsisters, Cinderella grew up
to be beautiful and kind.

Her stepsisters, for all their fine
clothes, lacked any beauty or grace.
This was a pity, because their mother
had great plans for them.

One day the king announced that he
was giving a very grand ball. His son the
prince was going to choose a bride.

Cinderella's stepmother saw that this was
the moment she had been waiting for.

"Henrietta, my darling! Georgina,
my precious!" she cried.

"Wonderful news! You're both
invited to the ball.

The prince is bound to fall for one of you
girls. What a wedding it will be!"

"But Mama, we haven't a thing to wear!"
screeched Georgina and Henrietta.

Nobody asked Cinderella. She was
made to work even harder.
There were no end of extra
jobs for her to do.

At last the day of the ball arrived.
How Cinderella longed to put on
a lovely dress and go to the ball!

Georgina and Henrietta enjoyed
teasing her.

"Don't you wish you could come to the
ball too, Cinderella?" said Georgina.

"Don't be silly," said Henrietta.
"Can you see anyone dancing with
Cinderella dressed in those rags?"

Cinderella said nothing.
She finished her work, helped her father,
stepmother and two stepsisters into their
carriage, and waved them off to the ball.

Chapter Three

Cinderella went back to the cold
kitchen, sat down by the fire and cried.
She was so very, very unhappy.

Wiping her eyes, she was surprised
to see a lady standing beside her.

"Oh dear me, tears down such
a lovely face!" said the lady.

"Who are you?" asked Cinderella.

"Your fairy godmother. I am supposed
to come when you really need me.
The trouble is, you have needed me so
much and I am only allowed one visit.
This royal ball is just the ticket."

"Oh, I'm so glad you came! I did so wish
I could go to the ball," said Cinderella,
"but it's too late now. I've nothing to
wear. My sisters would be furious if
I even touched one of their dresses."

"Stuff and nonsense!" said her
fairy godmother. "We don't want
borrowed clothes or carriages!"
She waved a magic wand.

There in front of Cinderella were
four beautifully wrapped boxes.
Cinderella opened each present
with great excitement.

But what strange presents they were!
A pumpkin, six white mice,
three fat rats and four lizards.

"Thank you," said Cinderella, a little puzzled. "They will make lovely pets, and the pumpkin will make a delicious pie."

"Pets and pies my foot!" said her fairy godmother. "Come into the garden. I've something to show you."

Chapter Four

Cinderella followed her fairy
godmother out of the kitchen.

Her fairy godmother waved
her hand over the pumpkin,
and there stood a golden carriage.
She waved her wand again and
the six white mice became horses.

Then the three fat rats were
turned into handsome coachmen
and the four lizards into footmen
dressed in scarlet.
Cinderella clapped her hands with joy.

"Well, my dear, your carriage awaits
to take you to the ball."
"I don't mean to sound ungrateful,"
said Cinderella, "but surely
I can't go dressed like this?"

"Oh silly me," said her fairy godmother.
"I nearly forgot the best part."
Suddenly Cinderella found herself wearing
the most beautiful dress, with a pair of
sparkling shoes made of glass on her feet.

"Just one thing before you go,"
said her fairy godmother. "You must
promise to leave the ball before
the clock strikes midnight.

If you don't,
all my magic
will vanish.

Don't forget,
leave before
midnight strikes.

Remember,
before midnight
strikes."

Chapter Five

At the palace Henrietta and Georgina
and all the other fine ladies met the
charming young prince. But oh dear!
The prince didn't want to marry
any of them.

Then a trumpet sounded,
Cinderella entered the room

...and the prince's heart went

BOOM.

The prince danced with
Cinderella for the whole evening.

It was magic.

"It's very rude of him," said Georgina.
"Fancy only dancing with her,
whoever she is."

"If I was wearing that dress
I know the prince would
want to dance with me,"
said Henrietta.

"She isn't half as pretty as either
of you," said their mother.

The prince was head over heels
in love with Cinderella.

She was as sweet and kind as
she looked, and he knew that
he loved her with all his heart.

All too soon the clock struck a
quarter-to-twelve. Cinderella could
hardly believe it was so late.

"Oh dear, I'll have to go! Thank you
for a lovely evening!" she cried.
"Don't go! Just one more dance!"
said the prince.

Cinderella was so happy she could
have danced until morning. But then
she heard the clock begin to strike
the hour…

"I'll be late! I really must go,"
said Cinderella.
"Stay!" said the prince.
"I want to ask you to…"

One... Two...

It was too late.
Cinderella was
already running out
of the ballroom.

Three... Four ...

As she ran, she lost one
of her glass shoes.

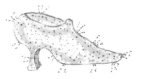

Five... Six...

She jumped into the carriage.
The coachman cracked his whip
and they sped away...

 # Seven... Eight...

...past the palace guards...

Nine... Ten...

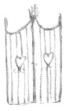 ...out of the
palace gates...

Eleven…

…just before the last note sounded…

Twelve…

Midnight!

Chapter Six

Cinderella found herself standing all
alone in the kitchen in her old rags.

Perhaps it was a dream?

But then she looked down and saw that she was still holding one glass shoe.

She quickly put it in her pocket.

A few minutes later her stepmother and stepsisters came stomping into the house. They were in a terrible mood.

"What a waste of time!" said Georgina, throwing her cloak and gloves on the floor. "That girl spoiled everything! It's not fair."

"Well, it won't do the prince any good
falling in love with her, whoever she is,"
said Cinderella's stepmother.
"All that's left of her is a glass shoe."

"He can't marry a shoe!" said Henrietta.

"Where's Cinderella?"
they all shouted together.

"We're hungry,
we want some tea."

"Tidy up this mess,
you lazy girl!"

And Cinderella came running
to do what they wanted.

Chapter Seven

The very next day the prince
announced that he would marry the
lady whose tiny foot fitted the glass shoe,
and that he would search the
whole kingdom until he found her.

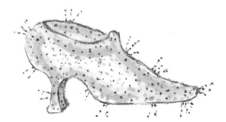

Cinderella heard this with
a sad heart, for she had fallen
in love with the prince.
Henrietta and Georgina had their
feet massaged daily and drank
nothing but rose water.

Each hoped that her rather large foot
would fit the glass shoe.

One day there was a knock at the door.
The prince walked in, followed
by a footman carrying the famous
tiny glass shoe.

"Me first," said Henrietta.
"No, me!" said Georgina,
kicking Henrietta.

"Ladies! One at a time please!"
said the footman.
Georgina went first.
She tried her hardest to squeeze
her foot into the dainty shoe.

She tried once, she tried twice,
she tried three times before
finally giving up.

Henrietta did no better.
There was no way her
big foot would
ever fit the magical shoe.

"Oh bother!" said Henrietta.

"Oh blast!" said Georgina.

"Oh thank goodness!" said the prince.

The prince was feeling sad. He had
visited every house where a young lady
was living, and he had not found his love.
Then Cinderella's father spoke up.

"I have a daughter, sir, who hasn't yet
tried on the shoe," he said.
"Please be kind enough to
bring her here," said the prince.

"You don't need to see her, sir,
she's a stupid good-for-nothing girl,"
said Cinderella's stepmother.

"But I would like to see her,
just the same," said the prince.

Cinderella walked into the room.
The prince saw a beautiful girl dressed
in rags, and he knew at once that
this was his princess.
He gently placed the glass shoe
on Cinderella's foot. It was a perfect fit.

"Impossible!" said her stepmother.

"It must be a mistake!" screamed Georgina.

"She's tricking you!" yelled Henrietta.

Cinderella took the other glass shoe
from the pocket of her apron…

70

...and at that moment her
fairy godmother arrived.

With a wave of her magic wand
she changed Cinderella into
a beautiful princess.

"Oh, I wouldn't have missed
this for all the tea in China,"
said the fairy godmother.
"It has turned out so well."

The prince took Cinderella
back to his palace. A week
later they were married, and
they lived happily ever after.

Snow White

 # Contents

For Shayane

Chapter One

One snowy day long ago, a queen
sat by her window sewing.
While she stitched, her thoughts went
to the baby she was going to have.

The queen pricked her finger on her
needle, and three drops of blood fell
on to the snow. She looked at the redness
of the blood, the whiteness of the snow,
and the blackness of the ebony window
frame and said, "I wish my baby's skin
to be as white as snow, her lips as red as
blood and her hair as black as ebony."

Soon after this the queen gave birth
to a beautiful little girl whom she named
Snow White. But happiness turned to
sorrow, for the young queen died.

The king was mad with grief.
He could not bring himself even
to look at his little daughter.

Snow White was taken away to
be brought up in another part of
the great palace, where her father
could not see her.

A year passed and the king married again.
His new queen was very beautiful and very
vain. Each day she would spend hours
looking at herself in her magic mirror.

Then she would ask, "Mirror, Mirror
on the wall, who is the fairest of us all?"

And the mirror
would answer,

"You, queen,
are the fairest
in the land."

The queen could not bear
to think that anyone was more
beautiful than she was.
What the mirror couldn't see
was the queen's heart, which
was ugly and cruel.

 # Chapter Two

Snow White grew up, long forgotten
by her father and hidden from her
stepmother the queen.

Snow White was very
beautiful. Her skin was as white
as snow, her lips as red as blood
and her hair as black as ebony.

Then one day the queen asked
the mirror her usual question.

It answered,
"You, queen,
may lovely be, it's true,
but **Snow White**
is far more beautiful
than you."

When the queen heard this she
turned pale with rage and envy.

She called for her huntsman.
"Take Snow White away and kill her.
Bring me her heart so that I know
she's really dead."

The huntsman took Snow White
to the edge of a dark forest where
bears lived and wolves howled at night,
but he could not bring himself to harm
this beautiful and gentle little girl.

"Run away from here, Snow White,"
said the huntsman. "Your stepmother
the queen wants you dead."

Snow White was so frightened that she ran straight into the forest.

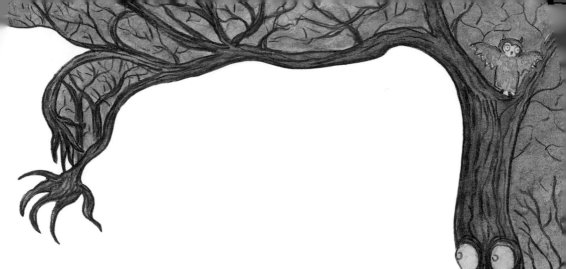

The huntsman watched her go.
Then he killed a young deer
and placed its heart in a box
to give to the queen.

"I won't be lying when I say Snow White is dead," said the huntsman to himself. "For no one comes out of the dark forest alive."

 Chapter Three

As Snow White went further into
the forest it grew darker and darker.

The trees tangled together and all
around her she saw the glinting eyes of
wild animals. Snow White was scared.
She fell and burst into tears.

But picking herself up,
she found to her surprise that
she was standing on a path which
led to the door of a little cottage.

"Maybe there's someone here
who can help me," she thought,
and she pushed open the door.

The lights went on and the fire began
to glow warmly. The strange thing was,
there was no one at home.

The cottage was neat and tidy.
In the middle of the room stood
a long table. On it were laid seven
little bowls and seven little glasses.

"Someone must live here," Snow White
thought. As if by magic all the bowls were
filled and wine poured into all the glasses.
Snow White was so hungry that she ate
some food and drank some wine.

Feeling very sleepy, she went
upstairs. There she found seven
little beds, neatly made.

She hoped that no one would mind
if she lay down on one of the beds and
had a rest. Soon she was fast asleep.

 # Chapter Four

This little cottage hidden away in the heart of the forest belonged to seven dwarves, who had lived there for as long as anyone could remember.

During the day they worked in
their diamond mine, and at night
they returned to their cottage.

Every night when they came home, the
lights would come on and the fire would
start to burn. Their bowls would be filled
with hot food and their glasses with wine.

Tonight, when they saw their little cottage, they froze. The lights were already lit.

"It's a burglar," said the first dwarf.

"Don't be silly," said the second.

They all went closer and pushed open the front door.

The food in the bowls was cold, and
one bowl and one glass were empty.

"It must have been someone,"
said the third dwarf.

"Food doesn't get eaten by itself,"
said the fourth dwarf.

"Maybe it was a bear,"
said the fifth dwarf.

The sixth dwarf went upstairs
and came rushing down again.

"There's a girl asleep in my bed!"
he said.

"We'd better go and have a look,"
said the seventh.

In the morning Snow White woke
to find seven faces looking at her.

"Who are you?" they asked.

Snow White told them about
her wicked stepmother.

The seven dwarves had heard of
the cruel queen and they were
very worried.

"The queen is sure to find out that Snow White is still alive and come searching for her," said one dwarf.

"Yes!" said another. "She is only little, like us, and we must look after her."

Chapter Five

All that day the seven dwarves
invented new things to keep
Snow White safe.

They fitted an alarm bell between
the cottage and the mine so that
Snow White could warn them
if she was in danger.

They built a pretend bear to
growl if a stranger was about.

And they made some traps
in case the queen decided
to come this way.

The next day the seven dwarves
set off for the mine.

"Be careful, and don't let anyone into
the cottage," they told Snow White.

The queen believed Snow White
was dead, so she was happy.

Her magic mirror was silent.

Then one day, she asked,
"Mirror, Mirror on the wall,
who is the loveliest of us all?"

The mirror answered,

"You, queen,
may lovely be, it's true,
but the seven dwarves
hide one more
beautiful
than you."

When the queen heard this she was angry.
She decided she must kill Snow White
herself. She could trust no one else
to do it. She made two magic potions, one
of them poisonous, and the other
for her disguise.

She dipped a red apple in the poison.
Then she boiled the other magic potion
until only a teaspoon was left.

Staring into her magic mirror,
she drank…

The queen began to shrivel and shrink,
wrinkle and wither. Looking out at
her from the mirror was the face
of an ugly old woman.

The mirror turned black and broke
into a thousand pieces.

The queen put on a magic cloak that would make her as invisible as night.

She put the poisoned apple in
her basket and set off for the cottage
where the seven dwarves lived.

Chapter Six

Today Snow White was planning
to make an apple pie. She was a very
good cook and she loved to help
the seven dwarves.

It was growing cold and snow
had started to fall, when she heard the
pretend bear growl a warning.

Looking up, Snow White saw an
ugly old hag standing in the doorway.

"Hello, my dear," said the hag.
"I have the reddest of apples
in my basket! Would you like one?"

"This old lady doesn't look anything like
the queen," thought Snow White.
So she let the woman in.

"I pass this way once a year," said
the old hag, "and I always leave
some apples for the little men."

"That's very kind of you,"
said Snow White.

The old hag took the red apple from her
basket and held it out for Snow White.
"This one is just for you," she said.

"Oh, it's so red and shiny!"
said Snow White.

Snow White took one bite
and fell down dead.

The alarm bell rang in the mine.
At once the dwarves rushed towards
the cottage.

The old hag fled into the forest,
but her magic cloak got caught in
one of the traps and she was forced
to leave it behind.

Now the queen was invisible no longer.
The dwarves chased after her as she
climbed up the slippery mountainside.

A wolf howled and the queen missed
her footing. She fell and was smashed to
smithereens on the rocks below.

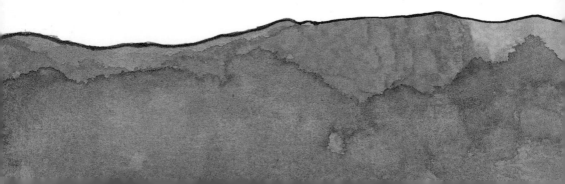

When the seven dwarves found
Snow White they were heartbroken.
They made a glass coffin,
with the words

HERE LIES SNOW WHITE,
A KING'S DAUGHTER

written on it.

Then they placed the glass coffin outside.
Ten years passed, and strange as it
may seem, Snow White kept growing,
and the tiny glass coffin grew with her.

One day a prince came riding by.
He had dreamt that his heart belonged to
a princess with skin as white as snow, lips
as red as blood and hair as black as ebony.
The moment he saw Snow White he
knew he had found her.

The dwarves did not want to part with
her, but they could see the prince
truly loved Snow White, so they decided
to give him her coffin.

The moment the coffin was moved,
the piece of apple which had been
stuck in her throat fell from her lips
and Snow White woke up.

"Where am I?" she asked.

"You are safe with me,"
said the prince.
"I love you with all
my heart."

He knelt on the ground
and asked his beautiful
princess to marry him.

Snow White looked into the prince's
eyes and knew she loved him.

Snow White wanted the
seven dwarves to be
guests of honour at her
wedding. Without them
she would never have
lived to meet her prince.

They all
went back to
the prince's
palace
together.

The wedding was
magnificent, and it is true
to say that Snow White
and her prince lived
happily ever after.

The Frog
Prince

Contents

For Maria Mirabela Ciobanu

Chapter One

Once upon a time there lived
a good and wise king.

He had seven beautiful daughters
and he loved them all very much.

One sunny afternoon the youngest
princess had nothing much to do,
so she went for a walk in the woods.

She sat down beside a stream
and began to play with her
favourite toy, a little golden ball.

She threw it high into the air.

She loved to see the way
it sparkled in the sunlight.

But she threw it too high
and it fell into the stream
with a splash.

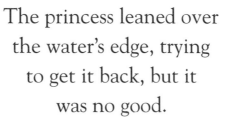

The princess leaned over
the water's edge, trying
to get it back, but it
was no good.

She started to cry.

"I would give anything in the world
to have my ball back again," she said.

Chapter Two

Just then a frog poked his head
out of the water.
"Croak! I can get your ball back,"
he said.

"All I want in return is the promise that I can eat from your plate and sleep on your bed, and that in the morning you will give me a kiss."

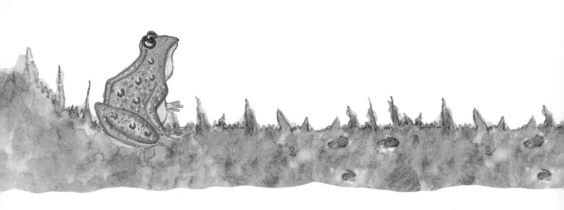

"Oh, how very silly this frog is,"
thought the princess.
"What use is a promise to him?
He will never be able
to leave this stream."

Feeling very pleased that it would
cost her so little to get her ball back,
the princess said, "If you bring me
back my golden ball I will promise
you all you ask."

The frog dived into the stream.
After a while he came up with the ball in
his mouth, and dropped it on the ground.

The princess was very happy.

She picked up the ball and ran home,
forgetting all about the frog and
the promise she had made.

 # Chapter Three

That evening the king held a party for his seven daughters. He had invited seven charming princes to keep them company.

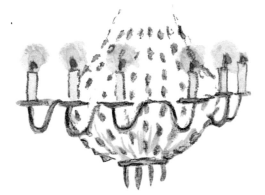

They had just sat down to eat when
there was a gentle knock at the door.

The princess ran to open it.
There, to her horror, sat the frog.

The princess felt very frightened.
She shut the door quickly and
went back to her chair.

"What's the matter, my sweet?"
asked the king. "You look pale."

So the princess told him what
the frog had said.

Everybody thought it was very funny.
Everybody, that is, except the king,
who was cross.

"You made a silly promise," said
the king, "and now you must keep it."

He asked the frog to come and sit on
the table next to the princess's plate.

The frog thanked the king
and began to eat.

The whole party watched with disgust as the princess shared her food with the frog.

Chapter Four

At the end of the meal the frog said
he was tired and ready for bed.

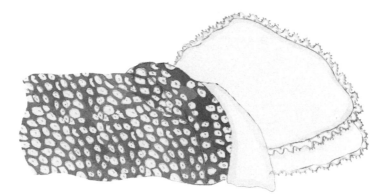

The princess did not want to touch him,
so she carried the frog upstairs on her
empty plate and put him down in
the corner of her room.

"You can sleep here," said the princess.

"No," said the frog. "I must sleep on
your bed as you promised."

So the princess put the frog on
her pillow and cried herself to sleep.

In the morning nothing would make
her kiss the frog. He didn't seem to mind.
He hopped away into the palace grounds.

"Thank goodness that's over.
I will never see that ugly frog again,"
said the princess.

Chapter Five

But the princess was
wrong.

"Crooaak!"

That night the frog
came back.
Again he ate from
the princess's plate,

and slept on her pillow.

In the morning he waited to be kissed,
but the princess couldn't do it.

The frog seemed to be growing
uglier by the minute.

"Crooaak!"

Chapter Six

On the third night the frog
was back again.

For the third time he ate from the
princess's plate and lay on her pillow.

But tonight as he lay there the
frog told a story of such magic
and enchantment that the
princess fell into a deep and
peaceful sleep. She dreamed
that she had married
a prince as handsome as the
moon and as bright as the stars.

In the morning when she woke,
the princess decided to get the kiss
over and done with.

The frog tilted his head for the kiss.

The princess, who thought this was
going to be really horrid, like taking
the most disgusting medicine,
kissed the frog.

And suddenly…

…the frog was gone, and the prince
from her dreams stood before her!

"Oh! What happened?"
cried the princess.

The prince bowed. "I was put under
a spell by a wicked witch," he said.
"Nothing could break it but a kiss from
a princess. I had almost given up hope
until you lost your golden ball."

The princess could not
believe her good luck
at having found such
a handsome prince.

"All I wish for now is that
you will promise to marry me,
and I will love you for ever,"
said the prince.

"This is a promise that I will
easily keep," said the princess.

The king was pleased when
he heard the good news.
"I know you will be very happy
together and I give you
both my blessing," he said,
hugging his daughter.

The next day the prince
and princess were married.

A very grand carriage with eight
fine horses took them back to
the prince's palace, and they lived
there happily for many years.

Sleeping
Beauty

Contents

 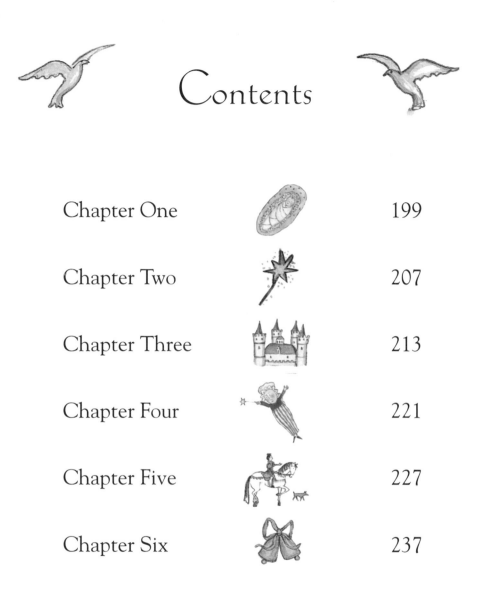

For Annie Maria,
to new beginnings

Chapter One

There once lived a king and queen
who had all they could ever wish for
except the one thing they wanted most,
a baby of their own.

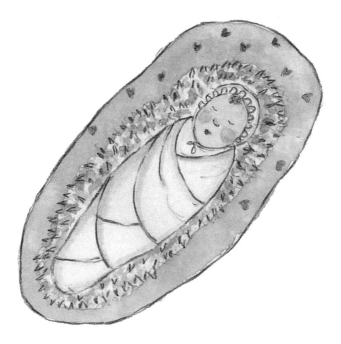

When they had nearly given up hope
the queen gave birth to a baby girl.
To celebrate their good luck,
they gave their daughter the
most wonderful christening.

They wanted the very best for
their baby, so they invited
the seven good fairies of
the kingdom to be godmothers.

Seven invitations were written but only
six handed out, for the seventh fairy
could not be found.

She had fallen out with her sisters,
locked herself away in a tower, and
turned her good magic into bad.
When the king heard this,
he tore up her invitation.

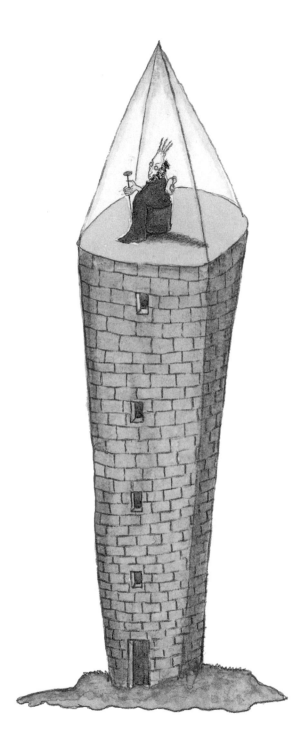

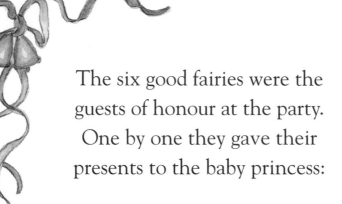

The six good fairies were the
guests of honour at the party.
One by one they gave their
presents to the baby princess:

Beauty,

Happiness,

Laughter,

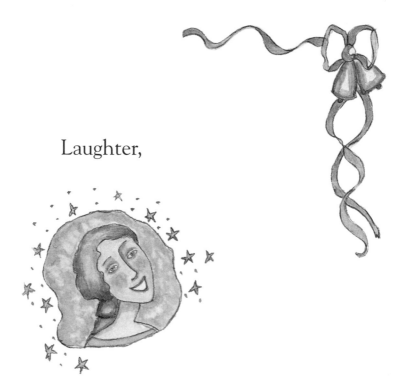

Wisdom,

And a voice like an angel.

Chapter Two

The sixth fairy was just about
to give her present when the doors
of the great hall burst open.

There stood the seventh fairy, face as
cold as frost, eyes as bright as fire.

She came near to the cradle, and
pointed a finger as sharp as a knife.

"I have a present for your precious
baby," she said. "Don't you want
to know what it is?"

"No!" said the king.
"Go away and leave us in peace."

The seventh fairy stamped her foot.
The castle rumbled.

The seventh fairy turned to look at the other fairies. "So, my goody goody sisters, what magical presents did you give the baby?"

"Will you please leave!" said the king.

"Leave! Leave!" yelled the seventh fairy. "I haven't given my present yet! When this baby girl is sixteen years old she will prick her finger on a spindle and she will die!"

"Arrest this woman!" shouted the king.

Soldiers charged in, but the seventh
fairy had vanished.

The queen cried, and everybody
was very upset.

Then the sixth fairy spoke.
"I cannot undo all that my wicked
sister has done, but I can make
sure the princess will not die.
Instead she will fall asleep for
a hundred years, until she is woken
with a kiss from a prince."

Chapter Three

From that day all spinning wheels
were banned from the castle
and the whole kingdom.

The princess grew up to have all the
things the good fairies had promised.
She was beautiful, wise, full of laughter
and happiness, with a voice like an angel.

She knew nothing about
the seventh fairy's present.

When the princess was sixteen, the king
and queen gave a birthday party for her.
As always with parties, there was a lot to
be done, so the princess passed the time
wandering about the castle playing with
her little dog.

Near her old playroom she saw a door she
had never noticed before.

"That's strange," said the princess,
opening the door.
She walked up some winding stairs
that led into a tower, where an old
woman sat at a spinning wheel.

"Don't be frightened, my beauty,"
said the woman, holding out a
hand with fingers as sharp as knives.

The princess went closer, for she
had never seen a spinning wheel before.
She sat down to spin.
At once, she pricked her finger
and fell to the floor.

The seventh fairy vanished…

...but her words rang out around the castle.

"The princess is sixteen and
have given her my present!"

Chapter Four

The king brought his daughter
down from the tower and laid
her upon a bed with covers
sewn with silver and gold.

The six good fairies
were sent for.

They went about their work
with great care, for they
could see the future
and they did not want
the princess to
wake up alone.

Soon the castle and everything
in it lay in an enchanted sleep.

The horses in
the stable,

the cat chasing
the mouse,

nothing escaped
the magic wand
of sleep.

To keep them all safe until
the hundred years were over,
a forest of thorns sprang up around
the castle, so thick that neither
friend nor foe could get through.

In time the castle and the
sleeping princess were no more real
than a story told to children.

Chapter Five

A hundred years later a prince from
a nearby kingdom was out hunting.

He came to the edge of
the forest of thorns,
and wondered what
lay behind it.

Giants?
Goblins?
Dragons?

He remembered his mother telling
him a story of a castle in a forest,
where a beautiful princess slept.

Her sleep would last for a hundred
years, until she was woken by
a kiss from a prince.

Suddenly the hedge of thorns parted
and a path appeared before the prince.
He walked through, and the wall of
thorns closed behind him.

The silence of a hundred years
lay over the forest. No birds sang.
The prince bravely went on until
he came to the castle, its walls covered
in brambles as sharp as knives.

The prince stepped over the
sleeping guards, and pushed open
the heavy castle door.

It was just like the story.
Everything lay in an
enchanted sleep.

He saw the cook icing the birthday cake,

a page boy stealing a chocolate,

a footman kissing
a maid,

a dog about to trip up the butler,

the butler carrying
a tray of glasses,

and lots of lords and ladies putting
on their finery.

235

All of them had fallen asleep
just where they were.

Chapter Six

At last the prince came to the room
where the sleeping princess lay.

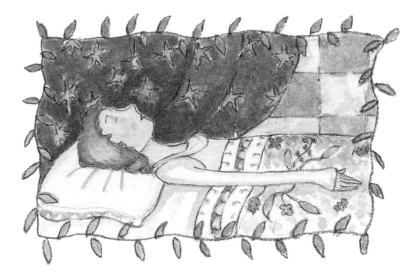

Never before had he seen such
a beautiful girl. She had lips as red
as roses, and skin as soft as petals.

He leant over and
gave her a kiss.

The spell was broken!

The princess opened
her eyes and looked
at him.

"Is it you, my prince? I have waited
such a long time!" she said.

The prince, charmed by these words,
lifted her off the bed.

The castle woke.

The cook finished icing the cake,

the page boy ate his chocolate,

the maid ran away from the footman,

the dog chased the cat,

the butler put the glasses on the table,

and the lords and ladies went
on getting ready for the party.

The prince told the princess that he
loved her better than he loved himself
and he asked her to marry him.

She had dreamt of him for
a hundred years and she knew
he was the prince of her dreams.

The king and queen were delighted
to find their daughter in love
with such a handsome prince.

The cook was a bit muddled.
Surely she was preparing for
a birthday party, not a wedding?

"You are doing both,
dear lady!" said the king.
"But let us eat before we
all die of hunger."

So the birthday party became a wedding
feast which lasted for seven days and
seven nights.

The prince and princess
lived very happily.

They had sixteen children and
their favourite story was, of course,
the story of Sleeping Beauty.

Early Readers

Your child's stepping stone from
picture books to reading books

To discover even more
Early Reader stories, visit
www.orionbooks.co.uk